Kai,
Always try your
best at everything
you do!
Brush, brush, floss, floss,
K-Masee

The Tooth Tickler

AuthorHouse™
1663 Liberty Drive
Bloomington, IN 47403
www.authorhouse.com
Phone: 1-800-839-8640

Published by AuthorHouse 05/21/2013

ISBN: 978-1-4817-5562-7 (sc)
*   978-1-4817-5563-4 (e)*

Library of Congress Control Number: 2013909337

Any people depicted in stock imagery provided by Thinkstock are models,
and such images are being used for illustrative purposes only.
Certain stock imagery © Thinkstock.

This book is printed on acid-free paper.

authorHOUSE®

"Josh!" my mom yelled from the kitchen.

I rolled over to look at my clock to see that it was 8am! "Why is my mom waking me up this early on my first day of summer vacation?" I thought to myself. I got out of bed and looked at my calendar. Oh yeah! It was my 6 month cleaning at the Tooth Tickler Dental Office. I ran to brush my teeth and wash my face. Then, I quickly ate my breakfast.

At the end of breakfast, my mom reminded me, "Josh, today is your little sister's first visit to see the tooth tickler, so you have to be a good big brother and help her through it."

"Yes ma'am," I answered as I went to get dressed.

Once we arrived at the dental office, my mother signed us in and asked if it were ok if Carly watched me have my teeth cleaned, since it was her first time. The office assistant agreed and the dental hygienist, Ms. Ruby, took us to the back. Carly's eyes lit up as she saw all the bright colors and neat things around her. I sat in the dental chair as my mother sat next to me holding Carly.

"Look Carly," said Ms. Ruby. "This is my special spaceship chair. Watch me take Josh for a ride. It goes up and down."

"Ooohh, this is fun," I said as Ms. Ruby moved the chair up and down. And then she let me back so that she could see inside my mouth.

"Ok Carly," continued Ms. Ruby. "I have to let Josh back so that I can see inside his mouth. I am going to use Mr. Sunshine as my light so that I can see." Ms. Ruby gave me a pair of cool sunglasses to block the light of Mr. Sunshine and turned on the light.

She picked up the mirror from her table and showed it to Carly. "This is my mirror. Can you see yourself in the mirror Carly?" Ms. Ruby asked. "This is what I use to look inside your mouth. Open wide Josh". I opened my mouth and Ms. Ruby looked around with the mirror. Carly clapped and giggled as she watched.

Ms. Ruby put her mirror down, picked up her explorer, and showed it to Carly. "This is my tooth counter Carly," said Ms. Ruby. "This is what I use to count your teeth and see how many sugar bugs you have in your mouth. Open wide so I can count your teeth Josh. The tooth counter makes a scratchy sound on your teeth," explained Ms. Ruby.

"Ok. I am finished looking and counting. Now I have to tickle your brother's teeth Carly!" Ms. Ruby said excitedly. Carly got excited and almost jumped out my mother's arms. She loved to be tickled. Ms. Ruby showed Carly the tooth tickler. "This is what I am going to use to clean Josh's teeth. This is my tooth Tickler! It goes around and around on all of your teeth and cleans off all the sugar bugs. Open wide so I can tickle your teeth Josh!" Ms. Ruby said.

"Carly!" I exclaimed after Ms. Ruby cleaned my teeth. "The tooth tickler sounds like my toy drill we play with at home!"

"Now, I have to wash off all the toothpaste from the tooth tickler. I am going to use my water shooter to do that. See my little water shooter Carly?" asked Ms. Ruby as she shot a little water across the room. Carly giggled again and clapped her hands. "Open wide so I can rinse your mouth Josh," Ms. Ruby said.

While she was rinsing, she showed Carly the suction. "This is Mr. Thirsty, Carly. He is going to take up all the water and toothpaste in Josh's mouth. You close on Mr.Thirsty just like a drinking straw and it makes a slurping sound."

"OOHH!" I shouted as Ms. Ruby finished rinsing my mouth. "My teeth feel so nice and clean, no more sugar bugs!"

"Now, I have some vitamins for Josh's teeth. They are going to make his teeth very strong. I just paint them on with this little brush. It feels a little gooey, but the feeling will go away in a short while. Open up so I can paint your vitamins on Josh," said Ms. Ruby. I opened and Ms. Ruby painted on my vitamins. "Ok, Josh, you are all finished. Now the dentist just has to come in to count your teeth once more with the tooth counter," Ms. Ruby said.

Then she looked at Carly and asked, "Carly, are you ready?" Carly grinned and clapped her hands. "Ride!" she exclaimed. Carly was ready to ride in the chair. My mother placed her in the dental chair next to mine as I watched and smiled. I was so proud of my little sister. She was having fun at her first visit to the tooth tickler!!

CPSIA information can be obtained
at www.ICGtesting.com
Printed in the USA
LVIC052109100613
337894LV00003B